Sunny Day, I overflow
My Werewolf girl I love you so
This book's for you my howling pro
I pray your wolf you don't outgrow

SLAUGHTER
A Werewolf Story
by Kristen Tomaru

Once upon a dark cold night,
I came upon a frightening beast.
Its claws were sharp,
Dark eyes sunk in,
Bloody jaws that smelled like yeast.

It had deep, bone rattling groans, you see,
And intentions quite well known.
My legs solidified with fear,
As its teeth, it proudly shown.

The ripples in the lake
Were clear,
The primal scene
Was set.
I ran as though my heart
Would burst,
My body drenched
With sweat.
I had to find a place
To hide!
My legs, they must
Move QUICK!
I collapsed beside a dark
Oak tree, and thought
I might be sick.

I closed my hands around my face
So my fear may finally cease,
Until I heard those dreadful sounds
Of **ripping piece by piece!**
The piercing smacks of tearing flesh,
I knew it was THE END!
Until I saw...
Within my grasp,
The mangled body of my friend!

I raked and ravaged through her corpse,
And thought...
"THIS JUST CAN'T BE!"
Within my bones I was the beast,
And in the beast was me.

My victims body pooled with blood.
The smell shook me to my core!
Her slaughtered limbs were warm and fresh,
And left me wanting more.

My body twisted
By the moon,
The hunt
Begins again!
I catch a flicker
Through the trees,
The shimmering watch
Of my best friend.
He was no match
For me, you see.
I had him on the run!
He would only cry
In pain
At the monster I'd
Become.

The froth streamed and foamed between my teeth
As we raced along the trees.
He SCRAMBLED as I snapped his leg,
And gnawed on both his knees.
My teeth sunk deep into his chest,
As his blood dripped down my chin.
I ripped and smacked and snarled black,
It soothed my beast within.

My fearsome bite would end his life,
It rattled his last breath.
He gasped when I bit through his throat
So near to his gruesome death.

The moon awakened in my bones
A bloodlust I can't ignore.
It tainted my sweet human soul...
A killer forever more.

Gruesome visions of my slaughtered friends
Walk beside me every night,

Their tortured screams will haunt my years,
The reminder of my plight.
My friends remains may ne'er be found,
Their bodies I've deboned,
By teeth and claws of this cursed hound;
Through moonlight they've been honed.

AHOOOOOOOOOOO
AH

OOOOOOOOOOOOOOOOOOOOOO....

THE END....

OF YOU?

9 781737 817413